SASHA SAVVY
Starts It Up

by
SASHA ARIEL ALSTON

Publisher
Gold Fern Press
Washington, DC

Sasha Savvy Starts It Up

© copyright: 2020 by Sasha Ariel Alston

All rights reserved. No part of this book may be used or reproduced or transmitted mechanically, electronically, or by any form other means, including photocopying, recording, or by any information or storage and retrieval system, without express written permission of the publisher.

Printed in the United States of America

Cover Design by Jana Rade

ISBN 978-0-9971354-6-6 (Hardcover)
ISBN: 978-0-9971354-7-3 (E-book)

First Printing: July 2020

DEDICATION

For you, who matters the most.
Thank you!

CHAPTER 1
NEW BEGINNINGS

Sasha Savvy wakes up, gets dressed, and heads down stairs to see what deliciousness her dad is cooking. When she gets to the table, it's wheat chocolate chip pancakes with strawberries, the cheesiest egg whites, and crispy turkey bacon. He never fails.

"I'm glad you can join us today," says Chef Steve Savvy.

Her older brother, Savion, snickers, and Sasha rolls her eyes. She's still feeling good though. Summer break is over and today is the start of middle school. Sasha's a sixth grader now, and she is so ready! She picked out her outfit last night to be super prepared.

She's wearing a white tee shirt that says "CODER" in black letters, a black skater skirt, and white-and-black Vans. And for the first time, her mom says she can wear a hot-pink lip gloss.

Her mom, Stacy Savvy, is dressed and standing by the counter drinking her coffee while checking her app on her phone that has all the latest DC tech news. She is a software developer.

"Hey, guys. Look at this. American University is having a hackathon for boys and girls from ages twelve to seventeen this Friday evening! Want to go? It's from five to eight," says Ms. Savvy.

"What's a hackathon, Mom?" Sasha asks.

"It's a competition where teams work together to come up with a project that solves a problem. Sometimes it involves coding."

"Nice! Coding camp was so fun again this summer. We learned more programming languages and made more cool apps."

"We knooow. You keep bragging about it," Savion snorts.

"Don't be rude to your sister. Sasha, I'm so proud of you. Remember how hard it was for you at first but look at you now. Glad you kept with it. Always more to learn."

Sasha has a huge smile on her face as she pops a sweet, juicy strawberry in her mouth.

"I'm down to check it out," Savion says matter-of-factly while trying to hide his phone on his lap to text his friend. Ms. Savvy made a rule that texting isn't allowed at the table during family meals.

"I want to go, Mom. Can I invite Gabby and Ashley?"

"Of course, you can. The more, the merrier. I will sign everyone up today."

"Wow! I'm surrounded by tech stars. I feel left out. Maybe, I should learn some coding myself. I need to update my website to include my new business," Mr. Savvy adds.

"I don't see why not, honey. Knowing how to code is important for everyone," says Ms. Savvy.

"Yes, Daddy! Do it! C.O.D.E. stands for Communicate. Organize. Demonstrate. Express. That's a trick Mom taught me to help me remember the steps to coding. I shared it with everyone at camp and they loved it!"

"Thanks, Ms. Instructor," he says as he gives Sasha a hug and takes her empty plate.

Breakfast is over and it's time for school! Savion gets dropped off first because Sasha's school isn't far from Ms. Savvy's job. This is Savion's first day at a new

STEM high school in Southeast DC. STEM stands for Science, Technology, Engineering, and Math. Savion is transferring there even though he spent two years at his old high school. He loves that there is a focus on STEM, but he was sad to leave his friends and his soccer team. Now he's cool with it because he realizes that he can still see his friends in the neighborhood after school or on weekends.

Ms. Savvy pulls up to the school.

"Have a great day, Savion. I can't wait for your report about your first day," beams Ms. Savvy.

"Bye, big bro!"

"Alright then. See y'all later."

As Ms. Savvy heads to Sasha's school, they listen to the radio.

"Alrighty, Sasha. Here we are. Your dad will pick you and Savion up after school. Have a great day, awesome sixth grader! Remember to listen, be confident and most importantly, be yourself!"

"Got it, Mom. Have fun with your meetings and stuff."

And with that, Sasha hops out of the car to go catch up with her best friends, Gabby and Ashley, to have the best back-to-school day ever.

CHAPTER 2

FIRST DAYS

Sasha texts Gabby and Ashley to see how close they are since she is the first one in their squad to arrive. Within five minutes, the two girls show up together.

"Hey, Sasha!" Gabby and Ashley exclaim.

Ashley's mom drops them both off since they only live three minutes from each other. Gabby's mom has a long commute and goes to work pretty early, and her grandma isn't feeling too good these days, so the moms have a perfect plan to help each other out.

"We're already in sixth grade, guys! Wow," Ashley gasps.

"I know, right? This is crazy!" Gabby says excitedly.

"Yep, so this means that we have to do something big! What are y'all waiting on? Let's go!"

Sasha, Gabby, and Ashley walk into their first day as middle schoolers. They are pumped. They are also happy that they are in the same class for first, second, and fourth periods. Although it's the first day of school, one of the teachers has to tell Sasha to stop talking a few times. She loves her friends and always has something to share, but she needs to remember to focus while in class and save the talking for breaks, lunch, and after school. It's so hard, but there is no way she wants her teacher, Ms. Davies, to call her mom.

At three-fifteen, the girls go to their school's aftercare program until Mr. Savvy arrives. He has to pick up Savion, so he won't be able to get them until three forty-fiveish. When Savion gets used to where his new school is located, he will begin to take the train and bus.

The main room is filled with many circular tables, and the walls are covered with posters of successful men and women who have made a difference throughout all walks of life.

"I can't believe we have homework on the first day!" says Ashley.

"We aren't little kids anymore, Ashley!" Gabby teases, and Sasha snickers.

"I loved the computer class. Mr. Cooper said STEAM instead of STEM though," says Sasha.

"Yep, the A stands for arts. I guess that's a way to show that STEM is creative," Ashley says proudly.

"Yeah, that's probably it," Sasha agrees. "Oh, I forgot to tell you. My mom told me about a hackathon on Friday that's gonna be at a college. It's this thing where you use creativity to solve problems or something like that. It's right after school and there's free food and prizes. Savion and I are going. Y'all want to go?"

"Count me in. If Savion is going, it must be pretty cool," Ashley adds.

"What about me? I'm going."

"Oh yeah. That too."

The girls look at each other and laugh while working on their first math assignment.

At three forty-three, Mr. Savvy parks behind a blue car to go inside and pick up the girls.

They get into the back seat of Mr. Savvy's classic, white Chevrolet Camaro while Savion sits in front.

"You like your new school?" asks Sasha.

"It was chill."

"Anything interesting happen?" Mr. Savvy probes deeper.

"I saw a few people I used to go to middle school with. Um, and for our welcome assembly, the owner of this new ed-tech company came in to talk with us. He raised one million to launch his startup."

"What? One million? I want to have my own business one day," declares Sasha.

"You can if you put your mind to it! You can be an entrepreneur like your dad," Mr. Savvy says proudly as he nods his head to a new rap song.

Mr. Savvy owns a catering business and is the author of a cookbook. And now he owns a restaurant. Over the summer, he opened a vegan soul food spot in the DC neighborhood, Capitol Hill. It's called Savvy Love. Things are getting pretty busy, but he still arranges his schedule to be able to pick the kids up on school days.

CHAPTER 3

THE NEXT STEP

The mayor of Washington, DC is having an event at Mr. Savvy's new restaurant. Unfortunately, this means that he will not be able to pick up Savion, Sasha, Gabby, and Ashley from school to go to the hackathon. Savion will have to pick up the girls.

This adventure will be new for Savion. He's taken the train before, but never to Sasha's school. His parents offer them rides as much as possible, or they do things close by. At his old school, he was able to walk home.

The teacher steps out of class, and Savion downloads the DC Metro and Bus app.

"Yo, Marc."

"What's up?" says Marc.

"You know how to get to Columbia Heights metro from here?"

Marc laughs. "Are you serious right now? You don't know how to go uptown?"

"Not on the train. Actually, I think I'll just call a ride."

"Bro, all you gotta do is take the orange line to L'Enfant Plaza and transfer to the green line. You'll get off six stops from there," Marc teases.

Savion just sits there with a blank stare.

"I get off at Georgia Avenue, which is the stop right after, so just get on the train with me and I'll show you."

Savion nods.

When they leave the impressive new building, everyone is outside waiting for rides, talking with friends, or walking toward the train and bus stops. Savion and Marc go to Eastern Market's train station. Ms. Savvy calls to make sure everything is going well. Savion assures her that he has everything under control. They take the elevator downstairs and patiently wait for the next train. Three, two, one, and a whoosh of wind hits them as the train passes to go to the end of the platform. A lot of the trains were upgraded with new navy blue seats and sleek black floor tiles with small white polka dots. Before you know it, they arrive at Columbia Heights at three fifty. Right on time!

Savion picks the girls up and orders a ride so they can arrive at the hackathon on time. Luckily, Ms. Savvy will be able to pick them up afterward. Savion sends a text to the family group chat and lets his parents know that they are safe and headed to the hackathon. The girls relax and enjoy the quick fifteen-minute ride.

CHAPTER 4

LET THE HACKING BEGIN!

They all get out of the car and thank the friendly driver, Justin, for the ride.

"Give that guy five stars. There was candy, bubble gum and water bottles in the back," Sasha comments.

Savion laughs and says, "I will, little sis."

They wait in a line at the registration table to sign in. As they walk into the big conference room, Sasha, Gabby, and Ashley realize that they are the only girls there.

"Are we supposed to be here?" asks Gabby.

"Yep. What's the problem?" Savion looks confused.

"Hellooo! We are the only girls here," says Sasha.

"The hackathon officially starts in thirty minutes. Chill. Give people some time to . . . I don't know, show up!" Savion sighs.

At four fifty-five, there is a burst of students who join the empty tables filled with swag bags. A handful of girls join. There is a folder with the schedule, a business idea list, a glossary of keywords, pencils, and a notepad.

A young woman walks onto the stage and grabs the mic. "Hello, everyone. So, who's here to solve some problems today?"

Some students scream. Some smile. Some keep talking.

Sasha whispers to Ashley, "I like her shirt."

It's bright orange with a purple robot on it.

"Me too. Is she gonna introduce the speaker?"

"I guess."

The students are still talking. The lady raises her hand as a sign for all the students to quiet down and pay attention. Finally, they do and focus their eyes on her.

"Alright! My name is Carla Thomas, and I will be your speaker today. Thanks so much to American University for having me. I know, for some of you, it's your first time attending an event like this, so pat yourselves on the back."

The girls lean in to focus. So does Savion.

Carla talks about her journey into the tech industry. First, she shares her success story of how she invented a fun robot named Kindnez that kids operate by using basic coding commands. She explains how if everyone works together, all kinds of problems can be solved, especially with technology. She goes on to say that everyone has the power to be a leader. Then she shows them Kindnez and how she works. Sasha smiles so big when Carla says, "Teach a girl to code, and she will change the world!" Sasha thinks that maybe one day she will change the world. She is so glad she came to the hackathon even though there are so few girls present.

There are tons of questions for Carla after her presentation.

Sasha raises her hand and asks, "Why do you think there aren't enough girls who are interested in technology?"

"Wow. That's a really good question! It's complicated. It can look like it is just for boys or so-called nerds, but that's not true. Those are just the images we see over and over on TV, in magazines, and other places. We need to make sure girls know they can do anything they want. We also need to include and support them when they show an interest in STEAM. Having events like this where girls like you are exposed to tech can make a big difference," Carla explains.

Sasha smiles and thanks Carla for her answer. She can't wait to talk to her mom about this later.

Savion gives Sasha a high-five for asking such a great question.

Sam, the planner of the event, says, "Alright! Let's give Carla a huge round of applause!"

Claps

"Okay, let's take a break so everybody can get food and meet some awesome people."

CHAPTER 5
INNOVATE

After a light dinner, it is time to get down to business.

"Today, we're going to do something fun and solve some important problems at the same time. We want you to get into teams of four and come up with a problem that you want to solve in your school or community. In your folder, there's a list of some ideas and a glossary of words that you can use to guide you," says Sam.

It doesn't take long before everyone scatters around the room to find partners for their team. The girls each go and look for groups to join, but each time the group says they already have enough people

on their team. They all end up back together at their table. Savion, who finds a group to join, looks over at the girls and sees them looking sad and decides to go back and join them. They are thrilled to have him on the team but try not to show just how much.

Volunteers pass out posters, markers, and magazines for inspiration. Sam gets everyone's attention to explain the instructions.

"Okay, everyone! Listen up! You will use the materials to create a slogan or design that describes the solution. Each team has one hour to make a poster and a pitch for the judges. Remember, a pitch is a quick presentation that describes what your company is, why it exists, and the goals. Some questions to think about while coming up with your idea are, who will benefit from this? What do you need to accomplish your goal? And what will be your biggest challenge? There will be volunteers walking around to help you," Sam explains.

"So, what are y'all thinking we should solve?" says Savion.

"How about we make special kits for homeless teens with things they need and some gifts too. Homelessness is a big problem," Sasha responds.

"That's a great idea, Sasha. Last week, my mom and I went to feed the homeless at this place called, Martha's Table. We and volunteers made over two hundred sandwiches and served them. It was really fun, and everyone was really nice," says Ashley.

"Oh, Wow. Good for you. My family volunteers there a lot," Sasha adds, not intending to one-up her.

"OK. Sounds good to me. I can sketch the design, while y'all think of a slogan," says Savion.

"Perfect. So, what should our name be?" Gabby says, jumping right in to get things started.

"It has to be something cool that doesn't mention being homeless. Something like, the Love Kit!" Sasha suggests with caution.

Ashley laughs and says, "What?"

"I mean, it does kind of make you want to know more about what it is," Gabby says.

"Thanks! Plus, we don't have much time," Sasha shouts.

"True. Sorry for laughing. Let's go with it," Ashley says, totally on board.

All of the teams are super focused while they listen to music in the background. There's a timer on the projector.

"I hope everybody has some amazing ideas for us! You have ten more minutes left," Sam announces.

In the last ten minutes, the Love Kit team discusses what they will say in their pitch. Their slogan is "Love Kit, one for all."

The first team goes up to pitch their idea. They want to create a club named FAMP for high school students who are interested in starting their own business in Fashion, Arts, Music, or Photography industries. The purpose is to provide students with the opportunity to make money by following their dreams while still in school.

Many of the teams come up with really clever ideas. One wants to have a scholarship app for students in foster care. Another one wants to provide low-income students with a home computer and free internet.

"Wow. These are some really great ideas!" says Gabby.

"I know, man. I hope more than one team can win," Savion says.

"Next up is table 8. Please bring your poster with you."

"OMG, that's us!" Sasha gasps.

Each team member says their name, and then in unison, they say, "We are the creators of the Love Kit!"

"Have you ever wondered what happens to the young people that are homeless, their environment, how they feel, and how they survive? Well, a Love Kit can show them you care. The Love Kit contains some basic daily necessities teens might need but may be difficult to get while being homeless. We have different kits for boys and girls. Of course, this does not solve homelessness, but we hope the kits allow them to have a few less things to worry about."

Sasha, Gabby, and Ashley describe what will be included in the kit and how this can be accomplished. They show off the well-designed illustration and their catchy slogan. The judges clap and look very impressed. The team walks off the stage feeling confident that they will be the winners of the hackathon.

The judges take fifteen minutes to discuss who the winner of American University's 3rd Annual Hackathon will be. Sasha, Gabby, Ashley, and Savion grow nervous while waiting for the judges to decide.

Finally, Sam walks up to the stage and says, "First and foremost, I want to say how magnificent each presentation was. These were, by far, the most well-thought-out projects we've seen since having the hackathon. Everyone was so bold. Although we had to choose one winning team based on our rules, I want you to know that you are all winners. Just coming here today, when you could have been doing any number of things, shows how motivated you are. With that being said, the winner of this year's competition goes to FAMP. We loved how nicely you developed the mission of the company, how creative and unique the poster was, and how much your pitch rocked given the short amount of time. Each of you will receive a fifty-dollar gift card and headphones from our sponsor."

The Love Kit team's mouths drop.

"Huh?" Sasha murmurs.

"What just happened here?" Gabby cries.

"Come on, guys! Have some team spirit. This was our first opportunity to gain some business skills. It's cool. We will do better next time. Let's congratulate them," Savion insists.

"Good idea. Even though we didn't win, we still had fun," Ashley pleads.

"You both are right. I just thought our idea was amazing." says Sasha.

"Me too. Oh well," Gabby sighs.

They go over and congratulate the winning team and then Sasha looks around for the speaker, Carla.

She sees her in the corner talking to Sam. She runs over to her and tells her thanks for coming. Carla says that it was her pleasure. Sam asks if he can take a selfie with the three of them. They all go into full selfie mode with the biggest smiles ever. Then Sasha finds Savion and the girls by the door.

"Hey guys, this horrible defeat calls for ice cream. I'll ask Mom to take us to our favorite ice cream shop when she picks us up. It's really close to here!"

"Perfect!" the girls shout in unison while Savion puts in his old headphones.

Unfortunately, Ms. Savvy says no to ice cream but tells them that she heard from Mr. Savvy that he has a treat waiting for them at home. The girls collectively sigh.

CHAPTER 6

BOSSES & CHEFS

Sasha and her besties arrive home and head to the kitchen. They all sit down at the long wooden Savvy kitchen table. Dad has a new recipe to share, and the girls are his favorite taste testers. He tries to make meals that are both delicious and healthy. This time, he is making dessert smoothies.

Sasha tastes first and makes a bad face. "Nope. Dad, this isn't ready yet. For one, it needs to be thicker!"

"Needs to be sweeter," Gabby says.

"Can you add more strawberries? And how about whipped cream?" Ashley requests.

"Hmm. Back to the drawing board," Mr. Savvy mumbles.

"Dad, this was not the best day. Our team lost the hackathon."

"Aw. Sorry to hear that, baby. I'm sure you did a great job. Better luck next time."

"No worries. We're gonna start a business just like you did. We discussed the whole thing on the ride home."

"Wow. That's pretty cool, girls. What's your business gonna be?"

"Hmmm, we haven't figured that out yet. Got any ideas?"

"Well that's up to you. You will have to brainstorm together as a team and try to come up with the best plan. You can think about the pros and cons. You know, the advantages and disadvantages of each idea," Mr. Savvy suggests.

"We know that, Dad. That's what we did at the hackathon."

Ms. Savvy comes downstairs and joins the rest in the kitchen and says, "So, what are you young ladies up to now?"

"We're discussing our business, Mom."

"Hmmm. Is that so? Great! I need an update. What is it?" Ms. Savvy asks excitedly.

"We didn't get that far yet."

"Well, think about solving a problem or making things easier for someone, and I'm sure you will come up with a great idea."

"How about a dog-walking business?" says Ashley.

"Or we can even start a chore service," says Gabby.

"We hate doing our own chores," Sasha chuckles.

They google kid business ideas, and most are taken. Sasha is frustrated.

"Well, it would be great if your idea was totally original, but it doesn't have to be. You can just find a different way to do something and make it better," Ms. Savvy confirms.

"Really? In that case, let's just do a lemonade stand," says Sasha.

"I did that before with my cousin. I want to do something different." Gabby insists.

"Yeah, let's keep brainstorming," Ashley suggests.

"Hmmm . . . let me think. How about selling healthy cupcakes?" says Sasha.

"You know, I love, love that idea," Mr. Savvy chimes in proudly.

"Everybody loves cupcakes. Grandma always says that she wishes there was a healthier version so she can eat as many as she wants," Gabby adds.

Sasha is glad that they have a business idea now.

"Hey, Dad, can you help us?"

"Yep, that would be my absolute pleasure."

"Dad, please don't get weird," Sasha says, because she thinks Chef Savvy is getting toooo excited.

"We need to come up with a special delicious and nutritious cupcake like nobody has ever tasted before!" says Gabby.

"We can start with three flavors and name them after us," says Ashley.

"I like that!" Sasha approves.

"Me too. This is gonna be big! We're gonna make a lotta money!" says Gabby.

"We will be famous!" Ashley declares.

"We're gonna change the world!" Sasha cries.

"That's all great, girls, but first, try these smoothies again," says Mr. Savvy.

Sasha tries a spoonful.

"Yum! Much better," Sasha shouts while doing a little happy dance.

CHAPTER 7

ROAD TO SUCCESS

The girls decide to name their business SAG Cupcakes because that is the first letter in each of their names, but Ms. Savvy suggests that they search the word sag to be sure that's a good choice. They discover that two definitions of sag are "to sink" or "to decline." This would be the worst thing ever to call their business if they want it to succeed. They are happy they didn't make that mistake.

"Well, what about SASHGABASH?" says Sasha.

Ashley and Gabby giggle.

"Aw, come on. This is the best way to combine our names."

They all start dancing around, saying, "SASHGABASH! SASHGABASH! SASHGABASH!" over and over again until it catches on.

"SASHGABASH it is!" Sasha settles it.

"So, what kind of cupcakes should we make?" says Sasha.

"I think we should have each of our favorite flavors as our own cupcake," says Ashley.

"Good idea! My cupcake flavor will be chocolate with vanilla icing and chocolate chip toppings," says Gabby.

"Chocolate chips aren't all that healthy," says Sasha.

"But the actual chocolate cupcake and icing will be. Plus, it will be dark chocolate. My aunt says that's the healthy kind."

"Oh, okay. Cool! I think I'll make a vanilla cupcake with strawberries on top," Sasha decides.

"Yum! That sounds delish. I'm going to make a red velvet cupcake with a cherry topping since that's a thing now," says Ashley.

"We can ask Savion to make us a logo so we can really be official!"

Savion walks in. "I heard my name. What's up?"

"We're starting our own cupcake business, so we

want to know if you can make us a logo design. Our business is called SASHGABASH CUPCAKES."

"Weird name, but yeah, no problem. I can whip that up quickly with a little bit of help with an app and Photoshop. Any special colors?"

"Pink," yells Sasha.

"Purple," yells Ashley.

"Yellow," yells Gabby.

"Okay. I got y'all."

"Thanks, bro. We appreciate it!" says Sasha.

"Actually. How about you make me the Marketing Manager so I can market and promote this business through social media. I'll make the social media accounts. The quicker we start building the SASHAGABASH brand, the better. Y'all can get the ball rolling with orders after I create a logo. How do the cupcakes taste?" Savion asks.

"We haven't gotten that far. We still need to make the recipe. We only came up with the name and what kind of cupcakes we're going to make," says Sasha.

"What? Sasha, come back to me when this is serious."

Sasha, Gabby, and Ashley spend the next two hours looking online and watching videos to see ways to make cupcakes healthy. They write down the main ingredients needed: white whole wheat flour, essential in each cupcake and unsweetened cocoa powder, to be used for the chocolate cupcakes. They talk over the recipe with Mr. Savvy and he approves. He also gives them a special ingredient to make the icing perfect.

Mr. Savvy then drives them to the grocery store to purchase the ingredients and items needed to make SASHGABASH cupcakes the best ever. Once they get back home, they start the baking process. Mr. Savvy shows them how to create the icing. The girls give it a taste test and they are more than pleased.

"Mmm, mmm, mmm! Dad, adding this to the icing makes it taste even better than a regular cupcake," Sasha says while licking her fingers.

"I know, right! You can't even tell that this is supposed to be healthy!" says Gabby.

"Thank you! With a little magic, everything can taste good, especially healthy things," Mr. Savvy adds proudly.

Sasha preheats the oven to 350°F. Gabby sets the alarm clock on her phone for fifteen minutes so she can remember to check on the cupcakes. After the cupcakes are baked, they let them cool down.

Next, the new chefs put the delicious frosting on top. Everyone tastes all three cupcakes and absolutely loves them! The girls are thrilled that their business is moving along. Savion gives them their props and promises to follow through with his marketing skills.

CHAPTER 8

WE'RE FAMOUS

"This is my sketch of the logo design I put together. What do you think?" asks Savion.

"This is pretty good but add a little more sparkle on the real one," says Sasha.

"Picky! I don't know how to do that. Let me go find out."

Savion goes upstairs and finds Ms. Savvy on the bed watching the news and scrolling on social media. She calls this multitasking.

"Ma, since you're the real MVP tech person in the fam, can you show me how to add sparkles to the logo?"

"Sure. Tomorrow."

"Maaa. We're on a roll now. SASHGABASH has momentum, so how about now," he insists as he gives her a big hug.

"Geesh. Okay, fine. Your hug is very persuasive. We'll use my laptop for this so you can try it on your own. In Photoshop, you will go to the Elliptical Marquee Tool to create a vertical oval shape in Layer 1. This is so we can have our own sparkling brush tool. Next, in the Filter tab, add the Motion Blur, set it to 90 degrees, and increase the distance."

Ms. Savvy wants to ensure that he is listening and understands, so she explains it step by step. Savion is writing everything down on his cellphone, using the Notes app, so he can try it himself afterward.

"Then, you repeat the same steps for the second vertical shape that you will create in Layer 2, but this time use the Gaussian Blur for a better effect. I'm making this shape thinner and longer because we're putting both shapes into one."

Savion nods as he tries to process this new skill.

"Once the merge occurs, rotate the second shape to a 90-degree angle so this can be used as a brush. In this case, I'll create a black background layer, so you can see the sparkling brush, but you will just put it on the logo design."

"Okay, cool. This sounds pretty simple!"

"Yep. Next, you go to the shape dynamics tool and the scattering tab to increase the size. If you need to make the brush size smaller, just use the left and right brackets on your keyboard. All it takes is a click and drag with your mouse to create the sparkles."

"Thanks, Mom! I'll try this now while I remember it," Savion laughs.

Savion goes back to his room and follows the steps. After a couple of tries, he successfully adds the sparkling effect onto the logo layer. With pink as the background, the logo has SASHGABASH in bold purple letters with the word CUPCAKES in yellow written in cursive underneath.

Savion goes to Sasha's room eager to share the new version with the team.

"Here's the logo! What do you think?"

"OMG. I'm totally feeling this!" Sasha can barely contain her happiness.

"Now we're ready to make social media accounts. Which ones should we get?" says Ashley.

Savion smiles. "I can set up accounts with Facebook, Twitter, and Instagram so you can target different audiences. We can make an online business account to process payments, but I have to wait for Dad to help me with that."

"Online?" says Sasha.

"Yeah, this is for people who don't have cash or prefer not to use cash to purchase your product once you start selling this in person," Savion explains.

* * *

Throughout the next two weeks, Gabby and Ashley go over to Sasha's house a few times after school to work with Savion on the marketing side of their new business. Gabby takes the photos, Sasha writes out the captions, Savion creates posts with quotes, and Ashley comes up with hashtags. Before they know it, all of their accounts have at least fifty followers.

"The followers keep coming!" Ashley exclaims.

"Wow. Let me go check it out!" says Gabby.

"Our hard work is paying off!" says Sasha.

Mr. Savvy walks in smiling as big as can be.

"Why are you so cheery today? Did something happen at work?" Ms. Savvy asks.

"You are looking at one of the next guests for Good Day, Washington. A friend of a friend is a producer there and enjoyed his experience at my restaurant. He wants to feature me on the show."

"Wow. Dad, that's so cool! You're really gonna be on TV?" asks Sasha.

Ashley's and Gabby's eyes widen, and they say, "Congrats, Mr. Savvy!"

The entire family is shocked, happy, and proud!

"There's more news. They want the whole family to be a part of it, and it's being recorded tomorrow morning!"

"Tomorrow? What will I wear? This is all so exciting, Steve! I knew Savvy Love was going to be a huge hit," says Ms. Savvy.

* * *

The interview recording the next day takes one hour to complete, despite the fact that the segment is only three minutes. The family sits down to watch themselves on the news that evening. Mr. Savvy mentions the girls' new cupcake business along with their social media handles. Savion checks one of their pages, and it's received three hundred likes.

"Sasha, I think it's time for you guys to do a launch event next month. People are talking about the business already," says Savion.

"I think that's an excellent idea," says Ms. Savvy.

"I'll talk with Gabby and Ashley to see what they think. That might be a lot to handle," says Sasha.

"Yes, but all of us will pitch in. You can have the launch at the restaurant. Just give me a date and I am ready," Mr. Savvy adds.

"Thanks for the support, Dad! We will come up with a plan. Just leave it to us.

* * *

During aftercare, Sasha talks to the girls about having a launch event. They agree to have it on November 1. The next few weeks, they spend time promoting the event through social media and creating flyers to pass around their neighborhood and a few other neighborhoods nearby. The girls even create buzz around school by getting the word out with their teachers and friends. Everyone seems excited for them and this is just the motivation they need. The girls are determined to have the best launch ever!

CHAPTER 9

START IT UP

Gabby and Ashley go over to Sasha's house after school to begin preparing for their launch event for SASHGABASH CUPCAKES. They head to the kitchen, where Mr. Savvy is placing all of the ingredients onto the counter. They need to make one hundred and fifty cupcakes by noon the next day, store the cupcakes overnight, and then add the icing and toppings one by one in the morning. The girls don't think that the cupcakes will be fresh that way, but they go with the flow. After all, Mr. Savvy, along with Ms. Savvy, are SASHGABASH investors and advisors.

"We have ten mini muffin pans that make twenty-four

cupcakes at a time. To make one hundred and fifty, we need to use about seven pans," says Sasha.

"Let's make a few more than we need, so we can try them," Ashley suggests.

"Cool, but we gotta get to work. We have less than twenty-four hours to make everything!" Gabby cries.

"Don't worry! We got this," Sasha says to be positive, but not totally sure if they really can pull it off.

While the cupcakes are being made, the Marketing Manager, Savion, is creating the poster banner and the menu for the launch.

"Hey, girls, how much are y'all charging for these cupcakes?"

"How about $1.50 each?" says Sasha.

"That's practically giving them away. Gotta be more. How are you going to afford to pay me, your best employee?" Savion wants to know.

"OK. How about $2.00?" Sasha suggests.

"Honestly, I think because the cupcakes are healthy and unique, the price should be $3.00. That's what this place called Fancy Cakes charges and ours are gonna be as good as theirs or better!" Gabby adds.

"That makes sense," Ashley agrees.

"$3.00 it is. We can start with that and change it

later if we need to," Sasha concludes.

Savion gets to work with the marketing materials, and the girls get to work creating their masterpiece cupcakes.

"Can you pass the flour?" Ashley shouts.

"Do you have the eggs, Gabby?" Sasha screams.

"I need the baking powder," Gabby yells.

Finally, the cupcakes are done. Everyone tries their favorite. Sasha and Ms. Savvy pick up the vanilla ones. Ms. Savvy goes first, while the girls watch.

She clears her throat and says, "I think you must have added too much flour," as she heads to the fridge to get some water.

"What?" Sasha says while taking a bite. "OMG! This is drier than dry! I ruined mine!"

"Dang, Sasha. I thought we all knew how to measure the ingredients," says Gabby.

"I know right. Our launch party is tomorrow!" sighs Ashley.

"I'm sorry y'all. I must have got carried away and added too much flour," says Sasha while she puts her head down.

"It's fine Sasha. We made them today just in case we had problems," says Ashley.

Everyone sees that Sasha is pretty down about the cupcakes, so everyone gives her words of encouragement.

"Thanks guys, but there has got to be a way to make sure the measurements come out perfect every time."

Sasha starts searching online and finds a tool that helps bakers make the best cupcake each time.

"Look, I found a solution. "It's an app called Bake and Create. It helps you make stuff without using a measuring cup. Instead of calculating the amount yourself, it tells you when you should stop or add more ingredients. We can use this to make our cupcakes."

"Even though your dad will say it's cheating, this is fantastic. Great find, Sasha!" says Ms. Savvy

"Thanks! Uh-oh. It says you need their special scale to use the app."

"I knew there was a catch," Gabby sighs.

"Not a problem, I'll go to Below Ten and pick it up. For now, just relax and download the app until I get back."

"Thanks, Mom. I appreciate it!"

* * *

Gabby's and Ashley's moms, Ms. Reyes, and Ms. Webster, arrive to prepare for the launch of SASHGABASH CUPCAKES. The event is from one to six that afternoon, so they show up at nine that morning to get to work.

"Let's get this party started!" says Ms. Reyes.

Gabby puts her head down in embarrassment. She thinks her mom always overdoes it with her bubbly personality, but everyone loves her.

Ms. Savvy laughs and says, "Super moms, let's head over to the restaurant so we can start setting up the decorations and putting logo stickers on the gift bags. We have a lot to do!"

"I'm up for the challenge!" says Ms. Webster.

Sasha, Gabby, and Ashley add the frosting and toppings to all of the cupcakes, and before they know it, everything is ready to be packed up to take to the restaurant. The girls, Savion, and Mr. Savvy get there at five after twelve. They spend the next hour setting up the cupcakes, adding more decorations and placing their business cards and a bottle of water into mini purple, pink, and yellow gift bags.

They wait and wait and wait some more. Sasha starts to think that no one is going to show up. Then

finally, she spots someone coming in. It's Ms. Davies!

"Our first customer! Welcome, Ms. Davies!" says Gabby.

"Hello, girls! Wowww. This is a nice setup. Can I take a few pictures?"

"Sure! Take as many as you like," says Sasha.

"Our decorations are a part of the experience!" Ashley includes.

Ms. Davies walks around to get a few shots. Within five minutes, a group of people show up and are ready to order their favorite flavor.

"Thank you for coming out today! How can we help you?" the girls ask.

"I would like to order one of each. It's wonderful to see young people doing something positive in the community. I know your parents are proud!"

The girls smile and grab the cupcakes that are already packaged. They have a display of cupcakes out so customers can see how they look.

"Thanks so much for supporting us," says Sasha.

The customer takes a bite. "Mmm, mmm, mmm! These are so good! I might have to grab a few more. I like that they're healthy too."

"Yes ma'am. We added a special ingredient so the

cupcakes can be nice and tasty," says Ashley.

Before they know it, it's three o'clock, and they have already sold half of the cupcakes. Savion is walking around taking photos to post on social media. A councilmember and Savion's friend Marc come too.

"Thank you, girls, for making a difference. You are showing everyone that kids can be entrepreneurs too. Good job, parents!" Councilmember Brown says in excitement while she eats a red velvet cupcake.

"I hope you enjoy it!" Sasha says while giving the last customer in line their special treat.

"How do you girls feel?" asks Ms. Webster.

"I feel wonderful. I'm amazed at all the love we're getting. I didn't know so many people would show up," Ashley says.

"Me either. Plus, a lot of people we know are coming out too," says Sasha.

"I know, right? I'm glad we have a little break though. I'm pretty worn out," Gabby sighs.

At five-thirty, they realize that they are out of cupcakes. Mr. Savvy removes the banner and poster from outside, so they don't attract any new customers.

"Whew!" Ms. Savvy falls into a chair.

"That was beautiful, girls! We're all so proud of you!" says Ms. Reyes.

"Yes, we are. Y'all killed it!" says Mr. Savvy.

"We couldn't have done it without each other!" says Sasha.

"What about me?" Savion insists.

"Yes, yes! You too, bro!"

The girls count the money they made, including the sales from their banking account that Savion created, and tips. The grand total is $550! They hug and high five each other and dance around in excitement.

Savion interrupts the instant party by asking, "Where's my cut?"

The girls look at him and burst into laughter.

"I'm serious."

"Son, chill. This is their moment. Their startup performance is stellar!"

"Huh?" Sasha asks. She and the girls all look perplexed.

"That means you guys did awesome! Congratulations!"

"Thanks, Dad," Sasha says while giving him a big hug.

"We should celebrate at the mall," Gabby says.

"For real! There's an outfit I want to get at Almost Forever."

"Before you go on a shopping spree, don't forget you will need to invest some of the money you earned back into your business. And if you are really gonna keep it up, your business will need to be registered. We can get into how later." Mr. Savvy says.

"That's right. Plus, you should save some of the money," Ms. Savvy adds.

Sasha thinks back to the speech Carla Thomas gave at the hackathon. She remembers how Carla said that girls can solve problems and change the world with technology. Sasha sees a connection between business, technology, and having a dream and a vision.

In a serious tone, she announces, "Hey, y'all. I think we should also make the kits for the homeless teens we talked about."

"Yesss! Now the Love Kits can have cupcakes too. It can all work together," Gabby says.

"Yep. People can also make donations for the Love Kits next time. Let's do it." Ashley adds, totally convinced.

Sasha can't hold back her excitement. "OMG, this is gonna be great! We can use coding and create an app that does everything we need to make this the best business ever. I love being an entrepreneur!"

GLOSSARY LIST

audience: a group of potential customers that the business chooses to focus on to sell their product

advisor: someone who has a lot of knowledge to help or give advice

brand: a name, symbol, or design that identifies you, your product or company from others

ed-tech: educational technology, technology whose primary purpose is to teach, inform, or raise awareness on something

entrepreneur: a person who creates and organizes a business

hackathon: a competition to create a project that will solve a real-world problem using technology

innovate: to introduce a new idea, method, or product

investor: a person who gives money or resources to a business

leader: someone in charge of a group of people or a business; someone who influences others to do something or someone who sets an example that is followed by others

market: to promote and sell products

motivation: a desire, want, or need to do something; it influences your actions to achieve a goal

performance: how the business is doing to reach its goals

pitch: a presentation that describes what the company is, why it exists, and its goals

startup: typically, a new small business or company working to solve a problem

vision: a clear guide of how you want the company to run

CPSIA information can be obtained
at www.ICGtesting.com
Printed in the USA
BVHW011646020922
646153BV00003B/14